Sneaking Suspicions

Elena's heart beat faster. Michael had been inside the pet shop a long time now. Too long. Something was wrong. She pushed open the dusty window and peered inside. Blackness.

"Michael," she whispered, "where are you?"

No answer.

"Michael, answer me. Are you here?"

Still no answer. Queer. Very queer. The feeling that something was wrong grew stronger as she swung her legs over the sill and dropped into the room. She left the window open for a quick getaway and began to look around. Where was Michael? "If this is his idea of a joke, I'll..."

She never did have time to finish her thought, because she was grabbed from behind, and a hand went over her mouth...

Mystery of the Plumed Serpent

Barbara Brenner

illustrated by Blanche Sims

Bullseye Books · Alfred A. Knopf
New York

Dr. M. Jerry Weiss, Distinguished Service Professor of Communications at Jersey City State College, is the educational consultant for Bullseye Books. A past chair of the International Reading Association President's Advisory Committee on Intellectual Freedom, he travels frequently to give workshops on the use of trade books in schools.

To Bill Hooks

Contents

Contents

Mystery of the Plumed Serpent

Prologue

First of all, picture in your mind two houses. Side by side. So close, they look as if someone had pasted them together. On the door of one house is the number 22. On the other is the number 24.

Number 24 is empty. The windows are dark. There must once have been a grocery store in the basement because there is a faded yellow sign over the entrance. It says GROCERY-BODEGA. *Bodega is the Spanish* word for grocery. *So now you know that this is a neighborhood where many of the people speak Spanish. That's all the empty house can tell us for now. But just remember—things change.*

There are lights on at Number 22. *Several families live here. But we're interested in only one family. The one on the second floor. Let's pretend to look in their windows.*

You see the boy lying on the floor with his

feet in the air and his hair over his eyes? He's called Michael García. He's reading. He's always reading. Especially books about Mexico. Maybe it's because his father, who died when Michael was a little boy, was Mexican.

That's Grandma over by the front window, in her favorite chair. From there she can watch everything that goes on in the street—and tell what she sees. Everyone loves Grandma; she's an old person with young ideas.

That skinny girl with the black braids who is slamming dishes around—that's Elena. Elena and Michael are twins, but they're very different. Their grandmother says, "Michael is a lake, and Elena is a volcano." That's not very scientific; it's just a family joke.

The twins' mother, Mrs. García, is the other person who lives in this apartment. She's the lady you see lying down in the bedroom. She's resting after a hard day's work in an office. She sighs a lot. You can understand why when you find out that she's a widow and has to take care of the whole family by herself, although Michael helps her with the checkbook (he's good in arithmetic), and Elena runs lots of errands (she's good at running).

There are two people you won't see tonight, but they're in this story. One is Fat Man, who always wears dark glasses. The other is Blue Jeans, who walks like a tiger. We'll meet these two tomorrow. So will Michael and Elena. And there's one character who will be there but the children will never see him—the Man with Binoculars.

But right now it's time for bed. The lights go out in Number 22. Now all you can see by the glow of the street lamp are the dim shapes of the two houses, side by side. When it's Saturday, the action will begin.

1 · Saturday

"I'm crazy about Saturdays!" Elena did a somersault on the living room rug in celebration.

Michael barely looked up from his book. "Why?" He was reading, but kept one ear open for any good ideas that might possibly come from Elena's direction.

"Because, dummy. No school. Saturday is the day when things happen." Elena rested her forehead on the rug and did a headstand.

From this new position she announced, "Today I smell adventure in the air." She had just read that sentence in a book.

"You smell the garbage truck down the street," said Michael, who always kept *his* feet on the ground.

Instantly, Elena sat up, her face flushing and her temper beginning to rise. "You know something? You're a deadhead. You never want to have any fun. You just sit and read your old books."

"And you're silly. You're always dreaming of things that will never happen," replied Michael.

They were off on one of those arguments that had no end and were so much fun when there was nothing else to do. The noise level rose steadily.

"You're a drag!"

"Dumb jerk!"

"Chicken!"

"Stupid dope!"

Grandma tried to ignore them. But after a few minutes she said, "*Madre de Dios,* I cannot stand it. Please make a little peace and quiet for an old lady. Go out in the sunshine and play."

Elena was willing, but she wanted company. "Well? Michael?"

"Well what?"

"Do you or don't you want to help me find an adventure? If you don't, I'll go by myself."

Michael put down his book, sighing. "I'll come. But you know nothing interesting ever happens in *this* neighborhood."

"You never can tell," Elena said brightly. "Adventure may be right around the corner."

Grandma was sitting at the window, listening. Now she joined the conversation. "Maybe not around the corner," she said, "but perhaps next door." And she pointed at something in the street below.

The children ran to the window. Sure enough, there *was* something. A big, red moving truck parked at the curb. Someone was moving into Number 24!

"You see. I told you." Elena was halfway out the door already. "I'll bet they're moving into the store," she called over her shoulder. Michael was close behind her. As they clattered down the steep steps, she asked, "Do you think it'll be another grocery?"

"Maybe it'll be a bookstore."

"I hope it's a dress shop."

"Well, whatever it is," Michael said, as they reached the door to the street, "remember, we don't have any money to buy anything."

"There you go again. So what? Haven't you ever heard of window shopping?"

And Elena skipped out the door and down to the curb. Michael followed, and in a minute they were both peering into the interior of the moving truck. It was very large and deep, and too black for them to see clearly what was inside. All they could make out were big square boxes covered with blankets. And then they began to notice the smell. There was a strange smell in the back of that truck. What was it? It reminded Michael of something. Of somewhere he'd been with Mama. But he never had a chance to think of what it was, because at that moment Fat Man entered their lives.

"Stand aside!" That *voice*. It was so soft. And it seemed to come from some cold place far away. It belonged to an enormously fat man who had come up quietly behind them and was now staring at them as hard as he could. At least they thought he was staring at them. It was hard to tell because he wore dark glasses. "There is something weird about having someone stare at you when you're not able to see his eyes," thought Michael. And Elena felt a funny chill down her back.

Fat Man spoke again, still in that soft, cold whisper. "Don't get in the way," he said.

That was an order! Then without another word, he turned and walked away. They watched him disappear into the front of Number 24. So he must be the new neighbor!

"What a grouch!" muttered Elena. They had retreated to their own front stoop to watch the moving men unload the truck.

Michael, sitting with his hands clasped around his knees, was about to answer when the first of the crates was brought out of the truck. In an instant they had both forgotten about Fat Man. All their attention was riveted on what looked like mysterious cargo.

But it was just about impossible to tell what it was. The crate was almost solid; there was only the thinnest space between each wooden slat. If the twins had been closer, perhaps they could have peeked through the slats. As it was, they could only look on curiously as, one by one, the big square boxes went into Number 24.

Whatever was in them seemed to vary in weight. Michael noticed that the moving men struggled with some of the crates more than with others. And he noticed something else. Each crate had writing on the side. And the writing was in Spanish.

By the time the fifth crate went past, Elena and Michael were getting restless. Just when they thought they couldn't stand the suspense one more minute, something happened. As the men were lowering one of the smaller boxes off the truck, the children heard a noise. A voice was calling from inside. It sounded very much as if the voice were talking about catching a cold!

Who can sit quietly on a stoop when wooden crates begin to speak? Elena and Michael couldn't. They dashed over to the crate and looked between the slats. And in a moment they were both laughing. There were no ghosts in that wooden box. It was a parrot!

With this discovery came a new idea. "I'll bet all these crates have animals in them," said Michael.

"*That's* what the smell was."

"It's going to be a pet store!"

2 · A Peculiar Pet Shop

Elena couldn't stand being on the outside any longer. She said, "Come on. Let's try to go into the store. Maybe if we offer to help them, they'll let us stay."

Michael wasn't so sure their help would be welcome. He remembered how Fat Man had looked at them! But Elena, who had already put that out of her mind, was determined. And she knew how to get Michael to do what she wanted.

"Just think of all those animals, Michael. Now the question is, do we go in or don't we? Are you brave or are you chicken?"

Michael, the head of the family, couldn't allow his courage to be in question. "Let's go," he said firmly. And they dashed over to Number 24.

The door was closed. When they pushed it open, a bell sounded somewhere in the back. They heard people moving around up in the storeroom on the second floor. And heavy objects were being slid along the floor. They heard a voice say, "Put them down easy. Don't drop them."

"They must be putting some of the crates upstairs," Michael said. And then they heard running footsteps and someone came down the stairs in the back of the store.

Someone new. A very tall man in blue jeans who took the stairs two at a time and

now stood blocking their way. Even in his faded workclothes he was an impressive figure, with his bushy hair and his thick beard. But the expression on his dark face was unfriendly.

"Sorry. We're not open yet," he said, scowling. "Come back tomorrow."

"Tomorrow's Sunday," said Michael quickly.

"Well then, Monday," Blue Jeans said, as though he wanted to get the talking over with as fast as possible.

Elena tried to be friendly. "We thought we could help you. And we might want to buy something. You want to sell things, don't you?"

Blue Jeans started to answer, but there was more sound from upstairs, and Fat Man came into view at the top of the stairs. He must have been listening because he said, "Let them stay." And he muttered to Blue Jeans over the banister, "We don't want people to get the idea we aren't interested in customers." Whatever that meant!

Blue Jeans stepped aside. But he kept a watchful eye on the twins as they looked around the store.

The moving men had begun to open the crates. Inside each one was an animal in a cage. For Michael and Elena it was like being behind the scenes at a zoo.

Michael headed for the snakes. There were two of them. They lay in one big tank, motionless and entwined with each other in the friendliest way. In fact, they almost looked like a single snake.

Elena didn't like snakes much, but she was fascinated by the monkeys and then by the lizards. A million questions were racing through her mind.

"I wish everyone around here wasn't so crabby," she thought. "It's a pain to have a pet shop move into the neighborhood and then to have the owners be so unfriendly. But I'm going to try to make conversation anyway." Then she asked, "Excuse me, sir, but could you tell me what kind of lizard this is?" She pointed to a green lizard that looked like a miniature dinosaur.

Blue Jeans frowned as if he didn't want to be bothered with questions. Then he seemed to remember that it was his job, and he said shortly, "A chameleon." Period. End of conversation. Elena saw Michael glance over at him, then look away again.

"Well, that's that," she thought. "That's all I'm going to get out of that Blue Jeans guy. That parrot talks more than he does." And she went over to look again at the big red parrot, the one which kept saying, "Catch a cold, catch a cold." She was about to ask Michael about the parrot when Fat Man came downstairs, and she heard Michael ask him, "What kind of snakes are these?"

"Very dangerous. The worst kind. Squeeze the life right out of you," Fat Man whispered, as if he hoped his answer would

make Michael leave.

"But what *kind* of snakes are they?" Michael repeated his question.

Fat Man hesitated an instant. "They're just snakes. Regular snakes." Then he said in his hoarse whisper, "We're locking up now. You better get out of here. Come back Monday." He was trying to sound friendly, but Elena and Michael got the message. Go home. Good-bye. Good riddance.

"I wonder if Fat Man is the owner of that store," Elena said when they were outside again.

Michael didn't answer. He was doing some wondering of his own. Now there's something you should know about Michael. Michael is one of those people who notice things. If something is odd, out of place, wrong, even if it's only a tiny detail . . . Michael will notice. It's as if a buzzer buzzes in his head. And at this moment Michael's buzzer was about to buzz.

Elena looked over at him. She saw him wrinkle his forehead, and she heard him say, "That's funny." Elena waited for a while because she always could tell when Michael was thinking something out. Then she said, to remind him that she was listening, "What's funny?"

"It's a funny place for a pet shop, our block. They won't get any business around here. Nobody in our neighborhood has money to buy pets."

"There you go again. Always thinking about money." But Michael didn't pay any attention to her. He was trying to figure things out. "And it doesn't seem like a real pet shop. They have no cages for sale. No dog leashes. No animal food to buy."

"Maybe they'll get all that later."

"And there's something else," he said finally.

"What?"

"Those two guys. They're not pet shop people."

"How do you know that, great detective?"

"Because they don't know anything about animals! Take that lizard you were looking at. Remember? Blue Jeans said it was a chameleon. It's not. It's an iguana. Anyone knows that."

Elena didn't see his point. "He could have made a mistake."

"Sure. One mistake. But not three," Michael said.

"Three? What do you mean?"

"You remember when I asked Fat Man about the snakes? Well, I know what kind of snakes they are. They're boa constrictors. And they're not really dangerous to humans. He didn't know the first thing about snakes!"

"I don't see. . . ."

"Elena," said Michael sternly, "any pet shop owner at least knows the names of his animals. There are over 200 different kinds of snakes, but there's no such thing as a 'regular snake.' There's something fishy about that place, and I don't mean in the fish tanks, either!"

3·A Newspaper Story

All weekend there was much coming and going at Number 24. Crates arrived. Crates were taken away. From Elena's bedroom, you could hear people moving around in the storeroom. Every sound made the twins more anxious to visit the pet shop again.

At last it was Monday morning, and Michael was saying, "Only six more hours."

And Elena was saying, "Six hours to waste in school. Ugh!" She sighed and snatched up a roll to eat on the way. Michael took the lunch bags. Mama began clearing the table so she could get to work.

Weekday mornings were busy in the García apartment. Everyone went somewhere. Everyone, that is, except Grandma, who took care of things at home. As usual she sat in her rocking chair by the window, reading her Spanish paper.

Grandma's reading of the paper was the high spot of breakfast time. There was something about the way she did it that always made you feel as if *this* day were going to be special.

She started the same way every morning. Reading to herself, moving her lips a little. Then she'd nod and say, "*Sí, sí,*" softly a few times. Or she might say, "*No, no,*" if she read something she didn't agree with. If she read something sad, she'd click her tongue and shake her head. Or if it were a funny item of news, she'd shake all over with laughter.

Michael and Elena loved to watch Grandma read the paper. But they knew better than to interrupt her. They knew that if they waited, very soon Grandma would suddenly slap the paper, as she was doing this very minute, and say, "Ha! Now that's a story!"

When she did, you could ask, "What is it, Grandma?" just as Michael was doing now. She answered, "Here is a story you *must* hear." They were already waiting impatiently for her to begin. She read, translating from Spanish to English:

"MEXICO CITY, *Mexico: The Mexican government is worried. . . . There is bad smuggling taking place across the border. . . . The smugglers dig up old treasure from ancient Mexico . . . from where they do not know . . . and they smuggle it out of the country. . . . It is sold to art dealers for much money. . . . The museum people say it may be part of the treasure called the Treasure of Montezuma. . . . The Spanish explorer Cortés left it behind when he went out of Mexico in 1520. . . . La Policía, the police of the United States government, help the Mexican policía to track down these thieves, and to bring the treasure back to the Mexican people."*

Elena sighed dreamily. "Now that's my idea of a story. It has everything. Mystery . . . action . . . suspense."

"And it's about Mexico," added Michael, as if that were the final test of a good story. "Boy. Imagine if we *lived* in Mexico. We'd have a real chance of finding something if we dug around. What would we find if we dug around here? Sewer pipes! Or the entrance to the subway!"

"Mexico, Mexico," Elena said. "Everything there is better. You're un-American, that's what you are!"

"Dope. Mexico *is* in America."

Grandma interrupted this exchange of insults. "And here is something else. It says . . . they think . . . the treasure is coming by airplane into New York City. . . . And . . . the Mexican government has offered a reward of five thousand dollars to anyone who has information."

"Five thousand dollars! Wouldn't I like to find those smugglers and get five thousand dollars!" Michael exclaimed. He thought of his mother and how hard she worked, and how much it would help her if five thousand dollars came their way. And here was a treasure, probably hidden somewhere in their own city. If only he could find it. "You're as bad as Elena," he told himself. "Don't let your imagination run away with you."

"Elena. Let's go. We'll be late for school."

"I'm coming. Good-bye, Mama. Good-bye, Grandma."

"Good-bye. Learn many new things." That was what Grandma said just about every morning.

The two children went out into the spring sunshine. They probably didn't learn much in school that day. But there are many kinds of learning. Their heads were full of iguanas, monkeys, snakes, Mexican treasure, and fat men with dark glasses.

As soon as they came home that afternoon, they set to work to find out as much as they could about the pet shop. Elena's job was to get back into the shop. "And keep your eyes and ears open," Michael ordered. She filled her pocket with food for the monkeys and headed for the pet shop.

"Aren't you coming?" she asked Michael from the doorway. She wouldn't admit it, but she was a little nervous about going by herself.

"I'll be down in a few minutes. I have to read something."

Shaking her head over brothers who are bookworms, Elena took off by herself.

There she goes, out the door. She is about to discover something—that treasure of one kind or another may be nearer at hand than one thinks. (Now that sentence has a hidden meaning. You may need to read it again.)

Just as Elena stepped outside, it began to rain. Hard. "Darn it," thought Elena, "that's bad luck. I didn't even bring an umbrella. I'd better make a run for it." And she scooted down the steps of her building, over to Number 24, and into the narrow entrance of the store.

The first thing she noticed was that there was a new sign where the old grocery sign had been. It said *Pet Shop*. "Pet Shop!" she thought. "I could have picked a better name than that. If I wanted people to come to my store, I'd call it *Jungleland* or *Wild World* or something like that."

"What if I didn't care if people came or not?" Elena thought. "Why . . . then I guess I'd call it *Pet Shop*."

Just then the wind blew the door open. The bell tinkled, and Elena stepped inside. She stood there waiting, but no one came.

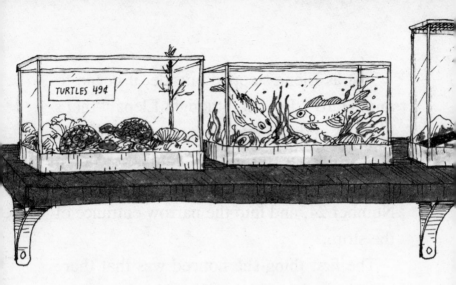

No one seemed to be in the store.

Elena was relieved. "Maybe they're up-stairs in the storeroom," she said to herself. "I'll just go ahead and play with the mon-keys." She looked around for a monkey cage.

They—somebody—had straightened up a lot since Saturday. Now the pet cages were in neat rows, and there were even some prices. *Turtles 49¢*, it said on the turtle tank. And the parrot cage had a sign that said *Parrot $20.00*. "Wow. You cost a lot of money,"

PARROT
$ 20⁰⁰

Elena informed the parrot, who promptly replied, "Catch a cold."

She giggled. "I probably will. I'm soaking wet."

Elena had to admit that the place looked more like a regular pet shop now. But there was still no cash register, no counter, and nothing that looked like pet food for sale. It seemed like a store, except that no one came to wait on her. But Elena didn't care. It was quite cozy in there all by herself, with the rain pelting down outside and with the animals for company. She began to think that she and Michael had had the wrong idea about the strange happenings of Saturday.

Now Elena located a big, screened monkey cage. "Hi! So there you are." She and the monkey struck up an immediate friendship. They soon understood each other. Elena knew that monkeys like to put things in their mouths, and the monkey soon understood that Elena would give him things to put in his mouth. She took out the fruit she had brought from home and began to feed it to him.

"There you go. Nice boy. You are really a cute monkey. I like you." She jabbered away, and the monkey jabbered back. She broke a banana in half and handed it to him.

"Here." The monkey popped it into his mouth.

"What? All finished already? Have the other half." The monkey finished the other half. Again he held out his hand.

"See. All gone. No more. What? You want the skin? All right, but it seems silly. Here." And Elena gave him the banana skin.

Now the monkey did something funny. He ran to a corner of the cage, scraped away at the paper and wood shavings on the bottom,

and hid the banana skin under it.

"Ha!" said Elena. "He's trying to hide it. Just like a dog hides a bone."

The monkey seemed to have other things hidden in his secret place. Now he pulled each one out, looked at it, bit it, looked over at Elena, then put it back. He was like a baby showing off his toys. Suddenly, he snatched something from under the paper, ran over to Elena, and held it out to her through the bars.

"Oh. You're giving me a present! Thank you." She grinned and held out her hand. The monkey dropped something into it.

Now what was Elena expecting? A nut? A piece of dried banana skin? A little marble? Certainly not what she saw lying in her palm!

4 · The Golden Snake

It was a tiny gold animal with glass eyes. It looked like a dragon with scales. Or were they feathers? Or was it a snake? Yes. That's what it looked like. A snake with feathers. How odd. How did it get into the cage?

Elena's first thought was that someone must have dropped it. "It's somebody's pin," she thought, "and the monkey's picked it up." But it had no clasp on the back. It was more like a tiny piece of sculpture. Actually, it was like nothing Elena had ever seen before.

"Anyway," she reasoned, "I'd better give it to the pet shop owner, if I can find him. Then the person who lost the pin can claim it." Elena headed for the stairs, the stairs that led to the storage loft on the second floor. She had gotten about five steps up when Blue Jeans appeared.

"Where do you think you're going? No one is allowed up here." He grabbed her arm in a not too friendly grip. And his face looked stern and frightening.

"Hey! Let go of me! I was just . . ." she stammered in her excitement. "I was just playing with the m-m-monkey, and I gave him a b-b-banana skin, and he gave me this. . . ." She was about to show the little gold snake to Blue Jeans when Fat Man appeared. She looked into his mean, pasty face, and—quite suddenly—she changed her mind. "The heck with him," she thought. "I'm not going to give him anything."

"Never mind," she said coolly. "It's nothing." She slipped out of Blue Jeans' grasp

and made for the door. Behind her she heard Fat Man ask, "What did the kid want?" And Blue Jeans answered slowly, "I don't know."

Elena breathed a sigh of relief. "Good," she whispered. "He didn't see the little snake after all!"

Dashing up the steps of her house, she ran into Michael.

"Oh, Michael," she cried breathlessly, "they—"

"Hey. What's going on? Did they do something to you?"

"Well, you see, I was going up . . . and Blue Jeans grabbed my arm and . . . Fat Man was watching and . . ."

"We'll see about that. They have no right to . . ." Michael was outraged. It was one thing for *him* to tease his sister. But let someone else lay a finger on her, and he was ready to fight.

"I'm going in there and tell them a thing or two," he fumed. He would have defended Elena to the death. After all, he was the man of the family. But when they got back to the pet store, it was locked! The shades were down in the windows. And there was a sign in one window: CLOSED.

"This store certainly keeps peculiar hours," Michael complained. "It's only four o'clock!"

"I don't care if they stay closed forever. I never want to go back in there." Elena shuddered.

Michael wrinkled his forehead thoughtfully. "There is certainly something suspicious about this whole setup."

"Michael, I have something to show you."

But Michael was so full of his own news that he didn't wait to hear Elena's.

"Listen," he said. "Today I found out

something. Did you know that every one of the animals in that store lives in Mexico?"

"So what?" Elena snapped. She was angry because Michael wouldn't listen to her.

"That *means* something. I'm sure it does. I just haven't figured out what it means yet."

"You have Mexico on the brain. While you were up there looking up that dumb piece of information, I was being scared half to death by those two—two—I don't know *what* they are."

"I don't either. But I know they're not pet store guys. Say, did you find anything suspicious while you were in the store?"

"I've been *trying* to tell you." And with that Elena told Michael about the monkey and the banana skin and the little gold snake with the glass eyes and how someone must have dropped it and how the monkey gave it to her and . . . " and here it is," she said finally. "I meant to give it back. But I got so scared and so mad, I didn't. And I'm not going back in that so-called pet store again. Ever."

But Michael wasn't listening to her. He

was looking at the little snake, and he had an expression that told Elena that his buzzer was buzzing again. He stood there for a few moments, turning it over and over in his hand while Elena fidgeted and said, "What is it? What's the matter with you?"

And at last Michael looked up at her and said, "This may be the answer."

"The answer to what?" Elena almost screamed. Michael had the slowest way of telling a person something. And Elena was the person least able to stand slowness.

"Don't you see?" said Michael, slowly and patiently. "Two guys have a pet shop. But they don't seem to know anything about animals. And they don't seem to want business. Why? Because it isn't their real business. It's a front—for another business."

"What other business?"

"Bringing something else in from Mexico. Something they hide in the shipments of animals. Something illegal; something like Mexican treasure! Maybe even Montezuma's treasure!"

"Michael! You mean Fat Man and Blue Jeans are *smugglers?*" Elena was willing to believe that they were bad men. But she couldn't believe they were that bad. "What makes you think so?"

"This." Michael held up the snake triumphantly. "I'll bet this isn't just a piece of junk jewelry from the five-and-ten. I have a hunch that this is real gold. And that those stones in the snake's eyes are real jewels! Elena, your monkey business may have given us a clue to the Mexican treasure!"

"Hey, wait a minute," Elena said. "If this is so valuable, what's it doing in the monkey cage? Haven't they missed it? Aren't they looking for it? How did it get there in the first place?"

"Not so fast. One question at a time. I figure it happened this way. They had the treasure box open, and it was near the monkey cage. These guys don't know anything about animals, so they don't know that monkeys are very curious. The monkey reached out and found something to play with. And they didn't even notice. They probably didn't miss it because it's small and because they must have so much more where this comes from."

Elena's head was whirling. Smugglers. Jeweled eyes. "This can't be happening," she thought. Already she was imagining herself telling the story to the police, capturing the thieves, collecting the reward, maybe appearing on TV, and. . . .

"We can't go to the police yet," Michael was saying, as if he'd read her mind.

"But why not?"

"We need real evidence."

"Isn't the gold snake evidence?"

"Maybe it is and maybe it isn't. But the police won't know if it's part of the treasure. We are not even sure ourselves. Besides, how do we know they'd believe a couple of kids? So what do we do?" Michael was thinking out loud.

"You tell me." Elena was impressed with her brother's handling of the case.

"First we're going upstairs and hide this in a good safe hiding place. And tomorrow . . ."

"Yes, what about tomorrow?"

"*Tomorrow* we take the gold snake to a museum. And we find out for sure whether it's part of Montezuma's treasure!"

5·A Trip to the Museum

"Hurry up, slowpoke. It closes at five o'clock."

Elena was impatiently shifting her weight from one foot to the other. She was telling Michael what he had already told her—that the museum was open only until five o'clock.

"Cool it." Michael was doing all the practical things, like getting the subway tokens ready, and making sure he had the little notebook in which he kept all the records of his "case."

But Elena couldn't be bothered with that. "Come on. Let's get going."

"Do you have the . . ." Michael lowered his voice . . . "the snake?"

"Yes. Right here in my pocketbook."

"Good. Then I think we're all ready." The children went into the living room to say good-bye to Grandma.

"And where are you two chickens going?" Grandma wanted to know. She liked to keep track of their comings and goings. After all, she was in charge while their mother was working.

"Don't worry, *Abuelita*," said Michael. "We're only going up to the museum to poke around." They had agreed to keep their mission a secret. But still, they hated to lie to Grandma. So they had agreed to tell her where they were going. But not why.

"That's a fine idea," Grandma said, nodding her head approvingly. "I'm sure you'll learn something there."

"I hope so," said Michael, and he and Elena exchanged looks.

So *adiós*. They were out of the house and down the stairs in a few seconds. And as they came out into the street, there was Grandma at the window, shouting last-minute instructions to them. "Come home before dark. Don't speak to strangers. Elena—keep yourself neat. And stop and get a carton of milk, will you?"

The twins stood on the sidewalk, smiling and waving. But suddenly Elena had a feeling that Grandma wasn't the only one who was watching them. She turned around. And there was Blue Jeans, lounging in the doorway of Number 24, watching. She poked Michael. They both began to walk away, fast. When they got to the corner, Michael glanced back over his shoulder. Blue Jeans was still there, looking after them.

"He's like one of those pictures where the eyes follow you no matter where you go," said Michael grimly. They both began to run, and they didn't stop until they got to the subway station.

"Let's slow down," said Michael breathlessly. "He probably won't be able to follow
us in here."

That was true. Blue Jeans didn't follow
them into the subway. But someone else did.
When they got out at their stop, there was a
man behind them. The Man with Binoculars.

And when they went up the stone steps of the museum, he was only a few steps away. But they never noticed him.

Elena and Michael looked very small as they entered the great hall of the museum. Michael took a careful look around and decided that the best place to find out what he wanted to know was at the desk marked INFORMATION.

"I have a piece of sculpture. I would like to find out how old it is. Who do I see?" Michael asked.

"Do you know where it comes from?" asked the man at the desk.

"I think it comes from Mexico."

"Then you want the Director of Mexican Studies. You're lucky. She's in today. Third floor. Room 310."

Up in an elevator that was like a little cage. Down the long hall where a huge mask of stone stood guard. Past the scale model of a Mayan village, where tiny Indians five inches high hunted and fished and cooked and worshipped their gods in a miniature world of a thousand years ago.

"Oh, Michael, look. Isn't it cute?" Elena would have liked to look around but Michael hurried her to Room 310. "Business Before Pleasure" was his motto.

They found the door marked *Director*. Michael knocked, and a voice said, "Come in." They opened the door and found themselves face to face with a lady who did not at all fit their idea of what a *Director* should be. She had on a big, broad-brimmed, Mexican peasant hat. Around her neck hung strings of brightly colored beads. And—this was the most startling part of her costume—over her shoulders was a huge blue and black cape, all made of feathers.

The combination of that exotic costume and the lady's gray hair and schoolteacher look was too much for Elena. She giggled. The lady, not at all angry, grinned back.

"How do you like my outfit? Things I found in Mexico. Just came back. Been there six months." Pointing to the cloak, she said, "This is all made of bird feathers. Can you imagine that? It's very old. Indian. Poor birds. I'm just wearing it for fun. It has to go on display. Well, what can I do for you today? Got something for me to look at?"

Elena and Michael were so fascinated that they could only stare.

"Come, come," she said amiably. "Haven't got all day. Let's see your arrowhead or whatever it is."

"It's not an arrowhead," said Elena. "It's a-a-"—she forgot the word—"thing!"

"Well, of course it's a thing. If it isn't a

person or a place, it has to be a thing."

"It's an object," said Michael. "We think it's a piece of sculpture."

"Let's have a look, then," the Director said cheerily.

Elena opened her handbag and carefully unwrapped the golden snake. She put it down on the Director's desk. There it lay, shining softly in a shaft of light from the window.

For a few minutes the Director didn't say a word. She just stared. Then she said softly, as if to herself, "Well, what do you know? A Quetzalcoatl. You've found a Quetzalcoatl." She picked it up and turned it over and over in her hand, then got out a big magnifying glass and looked at it through that. Then she leaned back in her chair.

"Well, now. That's quite a find. Yes, sir, quite a find. It's certainly old, probably pre-Columbian. That means before Columbus. Gold. And I think the eyes are jade; I'll have to check that. I would suspect that it's Aztec. Do you know about Quetzalcoatl?" she asked in the tone of someone who's about to tell a story.

Quetzalcoatl. Quetzalcoatl. (She pronounced it KEH-TZOL-KOTL.) Where had they heard that name before?

"The Quetzalcoatl is an ancient symbol in Mexico. It represents a god who took the form of a plumed serpent—a feathered snake. The Mexican Indians—the Mayas, Toltecs, and Aztecs—used to put it on buildings, in paintings, and in objects like this. But I've never seen such a beautiful one. Where did you get it?"

Elena started to speak, but Michael poked her.

"It's a long story," said Michael politely.

"I'll wait," the Director said.

"Be cagey," thought Michael. "Don't lie but don't give it away."

"You see," Michael began, "er—we found it. That is, a friend of ours found it."

"Your friend must have been in Mexico."

"Yes, that's just where he was. In Mexico."

"Did your friend report it? I hope so, because it is illegal to take valuable artifacts out of Mexico."

Now they were in a spot. Michael was flustered to be caught in his own lie.

As always, Elena plunged ahead.

"You see," she explained, "he wasn't exactly a human friend."

"Then what was he?"

"A monkey. There was this monkey who came from Mexico, and he gave it to me. That is, to me and Michael."

"Indeed," said the Director sarcastically.

"And what did you give him?"

"I gave him—er—a banana skin."

The more Elena told the truth, the more ridiculous it sounded and the redder her face turned.

The Director had heard enough. Suddenly she jumped up and said, "You wait here. I'll be right back." And she went into another room and closed the door. They could hear her speaking to someone on the telephone.

Elena and Michael didn't need to be told what she was doing.

"She's on to us," Elena hissed as she snatched up the snake and stuffed it into her pocketbook. "Let's get out of here." Without another word, they ran. They raced down the stairs and through the big entrance hall. They hadn't even noticed the guard signaling them to walk, not run. Nor had they noticed the Man with Binoculars, who had been standing outside the Director's office.

"I'll bet that Director called the cops," Michael panted. "They'll be looking for us."

"Maybe we should split up," said Elena.

"No," said Michael, firmly. "I promised Grandma I would take care of you."

That sounded brave, but the truth was that Michael wasn't happy about going home alone.

"I think we should go straight to the police," Elena said.

"No. We've only got one piece of evidence. It's not enough. I want to solve the whole case and then go to the police." Michael was thinking of the reward!

"You're wrong. We've got to do something now. If the smugglers find out we have the gold snake, we're liable to find ourselves in bad trouble!"

They argued strategy right up to the subway entrance. But once they got on the train, they didn't have much chance to talk. It was rush hour, and the subway was a sea of faces. One of them belonged to the Man with Binoculars. But of course they never noticed him. Elena clasped her pocketbook tightly, and every once in a while she felt for the shape of the golden snake inside. They were pushed and jostled and shoved. Sometimes they were separated.

At last they were at their stop and walking up the subway steps. It was almost dark. They were late! They hurried as fast as they could through the deepening twilight. Finally they were going up the steps and coming into the kitchen to the good smell of chili and rice and fried bananas. And the sound of Grandma scolding them because they had forgotten the milk and of Mama asking them if they had had a nice time. Michael gave Mama the change from the money they had spent while Elena went into the bedroom to put away her pocketbook.

In a few minutes, Michael joined her.

"Give me the snake, and I'll hide it in my bottom drawer. That's the one with the mothballs. No one ever opens that drawer."

"Sure." Elena reached into her pocketbook and—

"Michael," she gasped, her eyes widening. "It's gone. THE GOLDEN SNAKE IS GONE!"

6 · A Locked Window

"It can't be!"

"But it is. Look." Elena turned her pock-etbook upside down. "A penny. Two bobby pins. Tissues. Subway tokens. That's all there is."

"I knew I couldn't trust you," Michael exploded. "The one thing you were supposed to do!"

Elena's eyes filled with tears. "But Michael—see how tight that clasp is? It *couldn't* have opened by itself."

Elena was right. Someone had deliberately taken the gold snake. Someone had bumped against Elena in the subway, opened her pocketbook, and lifted it out. But how had the person known that Elena had the golden snake? Who could it have been?

The twins sat on the edge of the bed and let the bad news sink in. It had to be someone who knew about the golden snake. They tried and tried to figure it out. Michael even made a list in his notebook.

1. Blue Jeans. He must know. He must have seen it in Elena's hand.

2. Fat Man. He must know by now.

3. The Lady Museum Director.

4. Person or Persons Unknown.

Elena looked over Michael's shoulder skeptically. She didn't have much faith in lists. "If it were Fat Man, we would have seen him. You can't miss him, even in a crowd."

She went on, "Blue Jeans was at the pet shop when we left for the museum. And I saw him down there when we got home. He couldn't have gotten there and back before we did and stolen it from me."

"That leaves the museum Director!" said Michael.

But the picture of that funny lady with her feathered cape picking Elena's pocketbook on the subway just didn't add up.

So they were left with "Person or Persons Unknown." Of course Michael and Elena didn't know about the Man with Binoculars.

"Elena, we're in trouble."

"What do you mean?"

"Suppose the museum called the police.

Suppose the police trace us here. And we don't have the gold snake any more. They'll never believe someone took it from us. We'll have to pay for it. Or go to jail. Or maybe both."

Elena had an immediate picture of both of them growing up in reform school. Working night and day just to pay back the money for the golden snake. And what would happen to Mama while all this was going on?

"It will break Mama's heart," Michael said sadly. "That's what it will do."

"And what about Grandma?" said Elena, crying now. "How do you think she'll feel, reading those awful things about us in her Spanish paper?"

Michael felt a little like crying himself. But being the head of the family, he couldn't. So he just bit his lip, hard. "I figure there's only one thing to do."

"I know! Run away!" said Elena tearfully. "We can go down the fire escape and go to the docks and get on a boat and. . . ."

"Are you kidding? That's the worst thing you can do. When you run, then it looks as though you're guilty. No. We've got to get into that pet shop next door and find the rest of the treasure. I'm sure it's in there somewhere. Then we can go to the police and prove that we're not the thieves."

"And how are you going to get in?" Elena sniffed. "Make yourself invisible?"

"The fire escape gives me an idea. I'm going out to take a look. There's a window in that second floor, and I'll see if I can reach it from the fire escape."

It took only a minute for Michael to get out on the landing and over the railing to the fire escape next door. And yes—there was a window that led directly to the storeroom on the second floor. But of course it was locked! The window was so dirty that he couldn't even see into the room. But he could hear the parrot somewhere in the storeroom murmuring, "Catch a cold. Catch a cold."

"Even the parrots are peculiar in this pet shop," Michael thought. "Every other parrot says, 'Polly want a cracker' or, 'Hello, baby.' This one says, 'Catch a cold!' "

He climbed back in the window to the bedroom where Elena was waiting.

"I don't think that window's been opened in twenty years. We can't get in that way."

"How about if we broke the glass?" Elena suggested.

"You get the dumbest ideas. We'd have everybody in the neighborhood over here if we did that."

Elena just went right on. "You could cut a hole with a glass cutter. I read about someone who robbed a jewelry store that way once. This man came along and without a sound just cut a hole in the window and reached his hand in and took out a gold watch. Of course, they did catch him, come to think of it," she added. But Michael had stopped listening. He was busy thinking.

Just then Mama called them to supper. But tonight the good cooking was wasted on Michael and Elena.

"What's the matter with you two?" Mama demanded. "Since when don't you eat chili and rice?"

"They probably had ice cream," Grandma said. "Ice cream to spoil their appetites —that they remember. But the milk—that they forget."

"What a bad scene," thought Michael worriedly. "Mama feeling hurt, Grandma angry, our one real piece of evidence missing, and a good chance we're going to be arrested. I have to get us out of this. I have to. I am the head of the family."

Supper was agony. It seemed like hours before they were back in the bedroom and Michael was saying to Elena, "Here's what we'll do. We'll have to risk one more meeting with Fat Man and Blue Jeans. We'll both go into the pet shop. Then you'll do something to get their attention while I run upstairs and unlock the window from the inside."

"Sure. Great. What am I supposed to do, stand on my head?"

"Don't stand on it. Use it. Do something that will keep them busy for a few minutes."

"Hey," said Elena, "I've got it." When she told Michael her plan, he said maybe there was hope for her yet.

The next day when they appeared at the pet store, Fat Man was there. But Blue Jeans was nowhere in sight. Fat Man greeted them politely in his cold, soft whisper, even if he wasn't exactly what you'd call friendly.

If he knew about the golden snake, he never showed it. He acted as if nothing were wrong. He even let Elena take a turtle out of the tank and hold it. But he kept his eyes fixed on both of them. There was no chance for Michael to move toward the stairs in the back of the store.

Then a customer came in. Fat Man went to wait on him, and Elena began to put her plan into action. As Michael made his way toward the stairs, Elena moved casually to the monkey cage. She decided that the best time was just as the customer was going out. But it seemed as if that customer would never leave! As soon as he did, Elena slipped her hand into the cage and opened the latch. In a moment the monkey was loose!

"Hey!" yelled Fat Man. "What are you doing? That monkey is out of his cage, you little brat! Catch him. Catch him! CATCH HIM!"

Have you ever seen a monkey who's loose? One that's frightened and is being chased? He screams. He runs around knocking into things and bares his teeth and swings on anything that's handy. Even if he's a *little* monkey, he suddenly seems like a very wild

creature. It's scary. And Fat Man was scared. Which was just what Elena had hoped for. The monkey swung from the light fixture and Fat Man tried to make him come down. Then the monkey ran along a shelf, knocking things over as he ran. And Fat Man, puffing and sweating, tried to get the monkey back into the cage.

Meanwhile, Michael had disappeared up the stairs.

Elena pretended to help Fat Man. She pretended to be sorry she'd let the monkey out. Secretly she was overjoyed. Her plan was working! At least it seemed to be working. Michael was upstairs. But had he opened the window? What if it were stuck? What if Blue Jeans were lurking upstairs? Why didn't Michael come down? What was taking him so long?

Now the monkey, shrieking, leaped onto Fat Man's shoulder. Elena almost burst out laughing. The monkey was about a tenth the size of Fat Man! And yet the man was terrified!

She began to feel sorry for him as he cowered in the corner saying, "Get him off me, get him off!" When she saw Michael coming down the stairs, she ran over to Fat Man and gently pulled the monkey off his shoulder. The monkey came to her and put his arms around her neck.

Fat Man glared at her with a look of pure hate. "Get out of here. I never want to see

either of you in here again," he whispered. He didn't seem to notice that Michael hadn't been there all the time.

As soon as they were outside, Elena asked, "Did you do it? Did you get the window open?"

"Mission accomplished," said Michael, extremely pleased with himself. They walked back quietly into Number 22.

That night they waited until everyone was asleep. Until there were no sounds but Grandma's soft snoring and the rumbling of the food trucks making night pickups down at the docks.

Then, "All clear," Elena whispered from the bedroom she and Grandma shared. Michael tiptoed in. He was dressed in dark slacks and sweater. So was Elena. Elena had insisted that they both dress this way. "We'll be harder to see," she said. Besides, it was more like a TV show that way. Elena felt you had to be dressed properly to discover smuggled treasure, and Michael for once didn't argue with her.

Their plan was simple. Michael was to go into the storeroom and search. Elena was to keep watch on the fire escape. Elena had argued, nagged, shouted, and complained about this arrangement, but Michael was firm. It was too risky for both of them to go in the storeroom. This way, Elena could run for help if there was any sign of trouble. Elena had finally agreed.

When they pushed open the bedroom window, Grandma stirred a little. "Sssssh!" It would be bad news if Grandma woke up.

"If I know Grandma, she'd want to come with us," Elena giggled.

A moment later they were out on the fire escape and had closed the window behind them. They stood for a minute shivering a little in the night air. They looked around. Not a sound. Not a light. The yard between their house and the one on the next block was empty. The windows of the houses across the yard were closed and dark.

"Well, here goes nothing." Michael swung himself over to the next fire escape and pushed up the window. "This," he informed his sister in a whisper, "is against the law. It is called 'breaking and entering,' " and with these words he slid over the sill and disappeared.

Elena settled down to wait and watch. Little did she know that in one of the dark windows across the yard the Man with Binoculars was watching, too.

7·In the Darkness

Michael stood for a moment in the dark. It was too black to see anything, but luckily his other senses were working for him. First he smelled the familiar furry smell that told him there were animals present. Now his ears were straining to hear every sound. As he began to move around, he heard the animals stirring. Something scurried across the bottom of a cage. A bird ruffled its feathers and peeped. And the parrot that talked mur-

mured, "Catch a cold, catch a cold," softly.

It's a funny thing. When you can't see anything, your hearing seems to get sharper. Like a blind person's. Maybe that's why when Michael heard the bird talking it sounded different from the way it had sounded before. *Catch a cold?* No. Not catch a cold. *Keh-tzol-cotl.* Quetzalcoatl! The bird was talking about the ancient plumed serpent! Michael was so excited that he wanted to run right out and tell Elena, "I know what that parrot is talking about!"

"No," he mused, "that isn't smart. I don't have much time, and I'd better look for that treasure. But now at least I know that someone here was talking about a Quetzalcoatl, and that the parrot picked up the word."

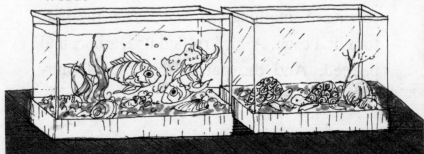

It was a good feeling to have another piece of the puzzle slip into place.

Now Michael dared to use his flashlight. He let the beam sweep around the room, then turned it off again. The light was too bright. You could see it through the window. But what could he do? He couldn't look around in there without light. He remembered a solution he'd seen once on TV. Taking his handkerchief from his pocket, he wrapped it around the flashlight.

"There! That's not so bright," he thought to himself. Then he began thinking it through. "Now, if I were two smugglers bringing treasure in from Mexico, where would I hide it? The most logical place would be in the packing crates used for shipping the animals."

Michael began a thorough search of the crates. He started at one side of the room and worked his way to the other. His flashlight poked inside each crate, searching out every dark corner and cranny. But there was nothing in the crates. In one corner there was an old office desk and a filing cabinet, left there by some previous tenant. He looked in those. Still nothing.

Michael was getting nowhere. He sat down on a dusty box to go over his situation.

"There's something up here that they don't want us to see," Michael thought. "Elena found a piece of treasure downstairs. The parrot says 'Quetzalcoatl,' so someone has been talking about a plumed serpent. They can't have moved the stuff out yet, otherwise they wouldn't care if we came upstairs. It's got to be here somewhere."

As Michael sat there in that dirty, bad-smelling, musty storeroom, just about ready to give up, he shined his flashlight on the biggest crate in the room—a tall one, which must have been used to hold a monkey cage.

Michael looked at it idly. And then he looked again. Something, something was different about that crate. What was it? He slid off his perch and went over to check. Yes, that was it. It was different from the others. It had a thicker bottom. Much thicker. Why? Why should one crate have such a thick panel in the bottom? Unless . . . Michael took out his penknife and pried around the edges of the panel.

"Hey! Look at that! The whole front comes off. There is a drawer inside!" A little more prying, and the drawer slid out. And there it was. *The treasure.*

And what a treasure it was! In his wildest dreams Michael had never imagined anything like this. When the flashlight beam struck the treasure, it seemed to light up the whole room. As Michael stood there, all alone, speechless, the words of a book he'd read came back to him. A description written long ago by a famous explorer who had seen part of the wealth of the Aztecs: *". . . the most lifelike copies of every created thing . . . whether on land or at sea, in gold and silver as well as in precious stones . . . so perfectly done that these seem to be the originals themselves. . . ."*

In his excitement, Michael forgot Elena waiting on the fire escape. He forgot about the smugglers, the police, the reward, everything but the piece of history that he had found. For a few minutes, it was 1520, and he was in Mexico. It was the *Noche Triste,* the "sad night" when Cortés, the explorer, and the Spaniards retreated from the Aztec capital city with their stolen loot. Bloody and defeated, they were unable to carry all the treasure with them. They threw some of their golden booty into the lake, left some by the side of the road, and struggled to their ships to sail away.

No one ever found the scattered treasure. Other cities were built on the lake and over the remains of the ancient Aztec city of Tenochtitlán. Finally, even the lake was gone, and all traces of the ancient city were covered by skyscrapers and highways and a capital called Mexico City. For over four hundred years, these things had lain under the earth until, probably by accident, someone had found some of them. And here they were.

Now Michael remembered Elena, waiting for him. Wait until Elena saw this! He snapped off his flashlight and started for the window. . . .

Elena was waiting. Waiting impatiently. And getting chillier and chillier. At first she had kept her mind on her work. Her eyes swept the yard below, and she listened for every sound. But after a while she couldn't believe that anyone in the whole neighbor-hood was awake, and she relaxed and let her mind wander a little.

"It certainly is queer the way things are working out," she thought. "Since last Satur-day, when I was so anxious to have an adventure, I've been having one. And it isn't over yet. I wonder how Michael's making out? That rat! Why do I listen to him? As usual, I have the bad deal, being the watch-man, while he goes into the creepy store-room and has all the fun."

Her mind went off in another direction. Supposing Michael finds the treasure and then the smugglers come, just as he finds it. Will they kill him? Will they make him a hostage? (Elena didn't know exactly what a hostage was, but she had heard the word somewhere, and it sounded like something nobody would want to be.)

Her imagination began working overtime, and she got very worried about Michael. So worried that she swung her skinny legs over the railing and listened for a few minutes at the window. When she didn't hear anything she went back to her post.

"I guess I would have heard if there was a fight," she reasoned. "Michael said he'd yell. It sure is cold out here. I really could use a sweater." She debated whether to go inside and get a sweater. She decided not to. She'd promised Michael to stay on the spot.

"I'm hungry. What I wouldn't give for a nice hot dog, with the works. And an orangeade. Or a pizza. The garlic kind. Or a meatball hero sandwich and . . ." Elena's mouth was watering. Better not to think about food.

"How much longer is he going to be? Say! What if he finds the treasure and forgets about me. What if he goes straight downstairs and out the front door of the pet shop and right to the police. But he wouldn't do that. Or would he? No. He wouldn't. He wouldn't do that to me. Not to his twin sister. Not Michael."

Now she began to think kind thoughts of Michael. "He really is a good brother. He takes care of me. He is really very smart. Look how he figured out about that gold snake. A good kid, even if he does fight with me sometimes. I would surely miss him if anything were to happen to him. Happen to him? What could happen?"

Now Elena's heart beat faster. Michael had been gone a long time now. Too long. Something was wrong. It came over her so strongly that her stomach gave a little lurch. *"Something is* WRONG. *I've got to go over there and get in that window. Michael is in there, and something is wrong."*

Elena stood up, took a deep breath, and

climbed over the railing. She pushed open the dusty window. "Breaking and entering," she thought fleetingly. "But I'm not breaking, I'm just entering." She managed to get the old window open and peered inside. Blackness.

"Michael," she whispered, "where are you?"

No answer.

"Michael, answer me. Are you here?"

Still no answer.

Queer. Very queer. The feeling that something was wrong grew stronger as she swung her legs over the sill and dropped into the room. She left the window open for a quick getaway and began to look around. Where was Michael? "If this is his idea of a joke, I'll . . ." she never did have time to finish her thought, because she was grabbed from behind, and a hand went over her mouth.

8 · Not a Moment
Too Soon

Strong arms pulled Elena across the room
and into a corner behind some wooden
crates. And then the hand came away from
her mouth, and a voice said, "Now don't
make a sound."

Blue Jeans!

In a corner behind one of the boxes was
Michael.

Elena was furious. "You," she whispered
accusingly. "You let me walk right into the
trap."

"If you'll pipe down a minute, I'll explain," Michael whispered. "Blue Jeans is on our side."

Blue Jeans motioned him to be quiet. "I'll explain. But I have to do it fast. They'll be here any minute."

"What's going on? Who'll be here?"

"The smugglers." Blue Jeans bent over and whispered urgently to her. "I'm Joe Bowler, a U.S. Customs agent. I've been on their trail for weeks. Finally got myself a job where I could keep an eye on them. I've been trying to hold off arresting them until we can find out who's buying the stuff and just where in Mexico it's coming from."

Now there was the sound of a door opening downstairs.

In an instant, Blue Jeans was giving directions. "I'm going to hide on the other side of the room. Stay here! And don't make a sound. Remember," he whispered, "whatever happens, YOU BE SURE TO STAY HIDDEN!" They nodded agreement.

Now there were footsteps on the stairs. There was a small clicking sound, and the lights came on. A smell of cigar smoke drifted up the steps. And they recognized the voice of Fat Man. Only now it was so oily and friendly it was hard to believe it was the same person.

"Right this way, Mr. Kane. I'm sure you'll find everything to your liking. It's the biggest haul we've brought in so far. Everything solid gold. And there's plenty more where this came from." He laughed a snickering laugh.

"This is how we bring it in. In the animal cages. We go right through customs, pay the duty on the animals, and no questions asked. Then we set up a 'front,' a store like this one, to throw people off the track. We don't bother much with customers off the street. We sell most of the animals to wholesalers. We get their names from the animal dealer who supplies us in Mexico. Of course, he gets his cut, too. As soon as we sell the animals, we're ready to bring in another shipment. And another shipment of treasure comes in with it!" He gave a wheezy little giggle, laughing about being so clever. He bent over, puffing, and pried open the drawer. "Here we are," he said proudly as the treasure came into view.

The man he had called Mr. Kane whistled softly. "Beautiful stuff. The real thing. Where do you get it?" he asked, casually. But Fat Man couldn't be trapped into giving away his secret.

"Wouldn't you just like to know, Mr. Kane!" he chuckled in his nasty way.

"Well, you can't expect me to buy without

knowing for sure if it's authentic Aztec stuff. I'll know if you tell me what area of Mexico it came from."

"Buddy, that's my secret. You want the stuff, you bid on it. You don't want it, someone else will. But where it came from —you'll never get that out of me."

Then Mr. Kane picked up one of the golden figures. It was a Quetzalcoatl, similar to the one that Elena had gotten from the monkey. Only this one was larger—about twelve inches long. It was obviously the prize of the shipment.

"That must be what the parrot heard them talking about," thought Michael.

"What are you asking for this?" Mr. Kane asked abruptly.

"Well," Fat Man looked at the end of his cigar, "I was thinking in the neighborhood of fifty thousand for the lot. That is, without the Quetzalcoatl. With the Quetzalcoatl, I'll say seventy-five. You know I split with the boys who dig it out and the agent who supplies the animals down there."

"I'm not authorized by my client to pay you more than forty."

"Don't give me that client business. You ain't got no client. I know you're the dealer. So let's cut out the kidding. Fifty thousand all together. That's my final price. Take it or leave it."

With this, Mr. Kane began to examine each piece of the treasure.

Fat Man said, impatiently, "All right. The whole shipment for fifty thousand. I'll put it in those bags over there. And make a list if . . ." The Fat Man broke off in the middle of his speech when he saw the open window. For a moment he stared at it. Then—"Hey! Who left that window open? What the . . . ?"

Blue Jeans sprang out from behind a wooden crate.

"All right. Stay where you are. You're both under arrest."

"Why, you, double-crossing . . . not me. You're not going to arrest me!" And Fat Man took a full swing at Blue Jeans, putting all his lard into it.

Blue Jeans ducked like a boxer. And the

fight was on! Fat Man was no match for Blue Jeans' fast footwork, and it would all have been over in a few minutes, if Mr. Kane hadn't sneaked up behind Blue Jeans with the golden Quetzalcoatl raised in his hand.

"Look out!" Too late. Blue Jeans went down, and Elena's yell had given away their hiding place. Fat Man and Mr. Kane turned and advanced on Michael and Elena.

The twins were paralyzed. Here came as much trouble as they had ever seen. And they were completely defenseless.

But when Fat Man lunged at them, he knocked over one of the reptile tanks. Out from the tank came six feet of boa constrictor, hungry for the mouse his sensitive smell-detector had told him was somewhere in the room. When Fat Man and Mr. Kane saw the snake, they panicked. Hurriedly, they began backing toward the stairs. That's when Michael and Elena, each of them pushing a crate, came running as hard as they could at the fleeing figures. They caught them right at the stairs. Down they went, backwards! *Crash!* Crates, treasure, everything went careening and tumbling down the stairs, to the cries of *"Oof!" "Ouch!" "Hey!"* And then came the welcome, glorious, melodious sound of a police siren!

When the police arrived, minutes later, they were greeted by the strangest scene they'd ever witnessed. Fat Man lay sprawled on the floor, still dazed from his fall. The parrot, which had gotten out of its cage in the excitement, was walking up and down the Fat Man's huge stomach, chattering, "Quetzalcoatl. Quetzalcoatl." Mr. Kane sat clutching a bag of treasure. His glasses were hanging half off his nose, and he was asking to see his lawyer. Blue Jeans sat on the steps, and

Elena was putting a handkerchief to his head, where a nasty lump was developing. Michael was trying to retrieve the snake, which had just finished swallowing a mouse.

The police rounded up the culprits and took everybody's name. Then they carefully

collected all the treasure. Michael and Elena tried to explain everything that had happened, but after a while they gave up and just told about the little gold snake they had found.

Blue Jeans was getting a headache and

seemed a little cranky. "What took you guys so long?" he kept asking. "A person could get killed waiting for you."

The cops said they'd come as soon as they were called, and it wasn't *their* fault that he had gotten knocked on the head.

Quite abruptly, it was all over. All the snakes, including the human ones, had been taken away to be locked up, the parrot had flown to a beam in the corner, Michael was making notes furiously in his notebook, and Elena, who was suddenly feeling tired, said, "I think I want to go home."

Three people climbed back across the fire escape into the Garcías' house that night —Michael, Elena, and their new friend, Blue Jeans (whose real name was Joe Bowler). They really could have gone through the front without waking anybody up. Grandma was already peeking through the curtains to see what all the commotion was about. She insisted on going into the kitchen to make them something to eat while they told her all about their adventure.

"Such smart children," Grandma said, when she heard how they had discovered that something was phony in the pet shop. And when Elena told her about the monkey and the gold snake, Grandma got so excited she began to speak Spanish. Then Michael told about the trip to the museum and how they found out that the gold snake was valuable.

Here Blue Jeans interrupted. "I suppose you wonder what happened to the gold snake. As soon as I knew that you were on to something, I telephoned my partner to tail you. He followed you into the museum and overheard your conversation with the Director. We were afraid you'd give the whole thing away before we were ready, so he took the golden snake while you were on the subway."

"And we never even knew it. Wow! If being on the good side of the law gets boring for him, your partner would make a great pickpocket," said Michael admiringly.

"But how did you know we were in the storeroom?"

"My partner was hiding in the house across the way. He was watching for the dealer and the smuggler through his binoculars. As soon as he spotted you going in, he phoned me, and I came right over. That's when I grabbed you, Michael. And later you, Elena. When he saw the lights go on, he knew that the smuggler had come to make a deal for the sale of the treasure. He was the one who phoned the police. I knew he would; I was just trying to stall them."

Now Blue Jeans stopped talking and looked at Michael. Michael was picking at the threads of his jacket with a soulful look on his face. "What's the matter, kid?" asked

Blue Jeans. "Tired?"

"No. I was just thinking about the reward. I suppose that you were working on the case first. So I suppose that means you get the reward."

Blue Jeans grinned. "Not me. Government agents don't get rewards. Besides, we never even got a smell of that treasure 'til you kids came along. You found the first piece. And you discovered where they had hidden it. I wouldn't be a bit surprised if the Mexican government decided to give you two that reward."

After that, they just *had* to wake up Mama. She had a cup of coffee and cried a little from fright and happiness. Elena joined her in the crying part. There was a lot of hugging, and everyone congratulated Blue Jeans. Which shows, as Michael wisely observed, how you can find new friends in the strangest places.

Epilogue

And so, the mystery was solved. The Mexican government got its treasure back, including the little golden Quetzalcoatl. And Michael and Elena did get the reward. But besides the five thousand dollars, the whole García family got an all-expenses-paid trip to Mexico, which they are going to take at Christmastime.

There was no question about the fact that the money took away a lot of Mama's worries. She stopped sighing and began to smile more. She told everyone how proud she was of the twins. But you must understand she would have been proud of them even if there had been no reward.

Joe Bowler went on to another case as soon as the bump on his head got better. He still comes around from time to time to see the Garcías. Sometimes he stays for dinner, and then he takes everyone to the movies. Michael is thinking of becoming a U.S. Customs agent when he grows up because he admires Joe so much.

And what, you may ask, did Grandma get out of the adventure? She got a great story, which the whole neighborhood will hear for many years.

There is only one part of the story that remains a mystery. No one ever found out where the thieves had been digging the treasure. But Michael says he is going to solve that *one when he goes to Mexico!*

*Now the block has settled back to normal,
which means that nothing ever happens there.
Number 24 is empty again. For now.*

But things change.

From the Author:
The Quetzalcoatl and Me

What makes an author choose a certain subject for a book? Why did I write a mystery about Mexico, snakes, and smuggled treasure, instead of about a spy ring or a mad scientist? The answer is that writers usually write about what interests them. And I happen to be interested in Mexico and snakes.

First, a word about snakes. I've always had a soft spot in my heart for these unpopular creatures. Maybe just because they are unpopular. Or maybe because they're such an old form of life. Or because so many stories and legends have been built around snakes. At any rate, I know snakes, and I like them, and I even keep a few as pets. One of my pet snakes is a six-foot boa constrictor very much like the one in *Mystery of the Plumed Serpent*. So, you see, it's not by chance that there is a Mexican boa constrictor in this story!

It's also more than chance that the Quetzalcoatl is so important to my tale. I first saw Quetzalcoatl on a postcard from Mexico City. I liked him at once because he was part snake. And I wanted to know more about him. So I went to the library and took out a book about Mexico. It didn't tell me much about my new friend Quetzalcoatl, but it told me some things about Mexico. Enough to make me want to know more. So I took out another book. And another. Soon, like Michael, I was reading everything about Mexico that I could get my hands on. And I was learning more and more about Quetzalcoatl.

It's hard to tell exactly when the worship of Quetzalcoatl began. But we know that he was an important god to the Aztec people about two thousand years ago. A famous temple still exists which is decorated with heads of a feathered snake, and this temple may have been built in Quetzalcoatl's honor.

Once Quetzalcoatl appeared, he was in Mexico to stay. But he didn't always stay the same.

Quetzalcoatl seems to have had the power to change form. As he moves through the pages of Mexican history, he is sometimes a snake-man, sometimes a king, sometimes a man-god. He is often the giver of life, other times the "lord of the wind." He even takes the form of an ant; one legend says that Quetzalcoatl could take the shape of an ant to carry the seed of the corn that would feed all his people.

One of the ancient kings took for himself the title of Quetzalcoatl, a sort of spokesman for the god. He said that the god liked round temples, and so he built a round temple to Quetzalcoatl. This temple became famous, and people would come from far away to see it and to make offerings to the great god. The remains of this temple are still standing.

The history of the Mayan Indians tells of a man-god called Kukulcan. (KUK is the Mayan word for a quetzal, a Central American bird. CAN is the Mayan word for snake.) This man-god, the story went, would arrive from the West. He would come from the sea, and he would be dressed in black and would have a black beard and a white face. Many historians think that this legend grew out of a real happening—the landing of Columbus on one of his voyages. Some Mayans must have seen him and passed the news along until the news grew into a legend.

Meanwhile, Quetzalcoatl in his many forms was painted, carved, and altogether deeply rooted in the history of the Mexican peoples. Later, when the Aztecs came on the scene, they adopted Quetzalcoatl and added him to their list of gods. They also adopted other things from the people who had been there before them—land, treasure, scientific and artistic ideas. Soon the Aztecs ruled a large part of Mexico. They built a beautiful island city which had hanging gardens, waterways, and a large amount of treasure, including Quetzalcoatls made of gold and jade and other precious stones.

By the time Montezuma II was ruler of the Aztecs, the Quetzalcoatl legend had become frightening. There would be a "day of judgment." Quetzalcoatl would come in his black clothes and black beard to claim the Aztec kingdom. He would come, it was said, in the "year of One Reed."

And so the stage was set. It was the year 1519, which was the year of One Reed on the Aztec calendar. A Spanish conqueror named Cortés landed on the shores of Mexico. He came by sea. He had a black beard and wore black. He was a white man. Everything seemed to be as the legend had told. When Montezuma heard of the coming of Cortés, he was sure that he was the great god Quetzalcoatl, come to take his kingdom. He quickly sent offerings of gold to the strange god. Since Cortés was no god but a greedy conqueror, the gold only made him more eager to conquer the Aztecs.

The story has a well-known ending. Cortés captured the beautiful city and put an end to the mighty civilization of the Aztecs. Montezuma didn't even put up a fight. How could he? He thought Cortés was the great god Quetzalcoatl! How interesting to think what might have happened if there had been no Quetzalcoatl. If it hadn't been for him, the Aztecs might have fought the Spaniards, they might have won, and the whole course of history might have been changed.

The Spaniards took as much of the wealth of the Aztecs as they could carry. They even melted down some of the beautiful silver and gold treasures so they could load them onto their ships in blocks. Other pieces they carried away as they were. Many were lost when the Spaniards battled their way out of the Aztec city later. Some of the treasure found its way to Spain. Some of it is now in museums in Mexico and the United States.

But now we come back to my make-believe story, *Mystery of the Plumed Serpent*. There is a mystery about the treasure of Montezuma. How much treasure was there? Did the Spaniards ever get it all? There is a legend about a great treasure that the Spanish never found, even though they tortured and killed the Aztec chiefs in an effort to find it. To this day, we don't know whether or not there is a hidden treasure.

That is the mystery. And that's the background of my story. But the story isn't finished. Someday you may read about a new find of treasure in Mexico. Someday they may yet find Montezuma's treasure. As we know, things change.

BARBARA BRENNER is the author of 40 books for young readers, including *Wagon Wheels*, a 1978 ALA Notable Children's Book; *The Gorilla Signs Love;* and *The Killing Season*. She lives in Hawley, Pennsylvania.